Marlys

Crazy Adventures

☆GALAXY ZONE☆

For Harrison, the kid with the constant smile! :) (Harrison

by Christy Harrison
illustrated by Avoltha

For Mom and Dad who laid a solid
foundation in my life

To Drew, the guy who can do anything

This book is a work of fiction. No part of this publication may be reproduced, stored in a retrieval system, or transmitted in any form or by any means, electronic, mechanical, photocopying, recording, or otherwise without written permission of the publisher.

ISBN-13: 978-1984003492
ISBN-10: 1984003496

Printed in the U.S.A.

TABLE OF CONTENTS

Chapter 1

No Time to Potty

"We're here! We're here! I can't believe we're finally here!" Marty shouted. As the school bus came to a stop, every child had their noses pressed to the windows in amazement. There before them was...

2

GALAXY ZONE,

the greatest amusement park of all time.

"Marty is ready to party!" he proclaimed as

he began to climb over the bus seats to try

to get to the front of the line. Mr. Brown, the bus driver, stood up and commanded, "Sit down, Marty! Since you can't wait and have some patience, you get to go last." Marty plopped down on the nearest seat.

While Mrs. Berry was handling the tickets, she told the children to go to the bathroom before they entered the park.

Marty was so excited to ride a rollercoaster,

he chose to skip the restroom break and head

over to the gate to see if he could see anything.

Shortly after, Mrs. Berry and the rest of his

classmates were entering the park.

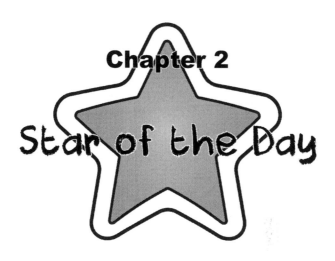

Chapter 2

Star of the Day

Once the children were divided up in groups of five, they were assigned to an adult for the day. Marty was placed in Mrs. Berry's group. "Mrs. Berry, can we go to the Laser Launch? I've wanted to ride it my whole life!!!" Marty said excitedly. "Marty, we're going to work our way around the park. We'll get to it eventually," Mrs. Berry replied. "Aww!" Marty whined. "Have patience, Marty. Good things come to those who wait," Mrs.

Berry encouraged. The first ride Marty's group came to was the Milky Way, an indoor rollercoaster. Marty was standing in line behind Benny and in front of Joe. However, that wasn't close enough for Marty. While his friends were talking, Marty snuck around Benny and cut.

Marty passed through the last entry way before getting on the ride. A worker was standing there counting people as they

stepped through. All of a sudden, when Benny stepped through, a loud buzzer went off and lights started flashing.

"Congratulations! You are Galaxy Zone's Star of the Day!" the worker exclaimed. "You have won $100 to spend in the park today and four free passes to return in the future."

"What?!" Marty shouted. "That was my place in line! That prize is mine!" "Marty, remember what I said?" Mrs. Berry interrupted. "Good things come to those who wait." "Yes, ma'am," Marty murmured.

Just then, Marty actually remembered something his mother had written down and taped to his door.

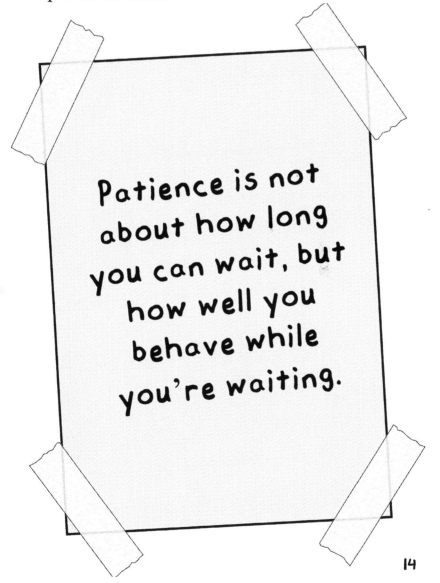

Patience is not about how long you can wait, but how well you behave while you're waiting.

Chapter 3

Star Fall Fail

After the group was finished riding the Milky

Way, they headed over to Star Fall, a ride

that drops you 10 stories. While standing in

line, Marty realized he should've gone to the

bathroom when everyone else did. He tried

to control it, but he just couldn't.

He began to sway from left to right, as beads of sweat began to form on his brow. The pee pee dance had begun. "Mrs. Berry," Marty said with a worried look on his face, "I think I need to go to the bathroom really bad!"

"Oh, Marty!" Mrs. Berry said with an eye roll. "Come on." "Marty! You're gonna miss Star Fall!" Joe exclaimed. "Yes, he is. This is what happens when you don't use patience and follow directions. Now Marty gets to ride the exciting 'Restroom Express' instead," Mrs. Berry scolded. As the two exited the line, Marty could hear screams of joy coming from the ride.

Chapter 4

Barf-O-Rama!

After riding two more rides, Mrs. Berry's group came to the Black Hole. "I love this ride!" Megan squealed. "It spins you around and around and around and around! Then

the floor drops down, and you stick to the wall!" "I'm starving!" Marty declared. "Well, we can break for lunch after this ride," Mrs. Berry said.

THE BLACK HOLE

Just then, Marty caught a glimpse of a sign that said, "GALACTIC CHEESE FRIES." Marty's mouth began to water, and his tongue started to tingle. "Mrs. Berry, please oh please, can I get some cheese fries and eat

them while we're waiting in line?" Marty
begged. "Marty, I really think you should
wait 'til after this ride," Mrs. Berry
suggested. "I'll eat them superfast!" Marty
said as he headed to get his fries.

At the food stand, Marty quickly ordered the large gooey galactic fries with extra cheese. "Sorry kid, you'll have to wait for the cheese to heat up," the worker said. "Aw, man! I don't have time to wait!" Marty said with a disappointed look. "Well, we have chili and onions as a topping. It's hot and ready," the man suggested. "Uh, ok," Marty said as he

paid him. He took off after his group as
fast as his legs would carry him. Marty was
cramming the hot gooey chili fries in his
mouth with every step.

Marty finished the Galactic Chili Fries just as they were about to enter the Black Hole. Everyone began lining up along the wall of the spinning cylinder.

"This is going to be awesome!" Benny

shouted. Just then, Marty felt an uneasy

rumble in his tummy!

The cylinder began spinning faster and faster. Marty felt his body being pressed to the wall. His stomach was doing flip flops. As he gazed around at all of the people laughing and screaming, he realized something terrible was about to happen.

Before he could warn anyone, Marty's Galactic Chili Fries decided to reappear and shower Marty's shirt and those next to him.

Warning: For those who have a problem looking at gross things, please skip the next page.

Mrs. Berry approached Marty and stared into his eyes. "Bad things definitely came because I didn't wait," admitted Marty.

Marty's group quickly decided to ride the Solar Splash next to try and clean off.

Chapter 5

On the Edge

"Man! The Solar Splash soaked me!" exclaimed Benny. "Me too!" agreed Joe. "But it's better than wearing chili barf!"

"Hey, look!" cried Lillie. "It's the Cosmic Coaster, the tallest ride in the park!"

"Yes!" screamed Marty. "Finally!" This was going to be Marty's first time to ride it. Last year he had been too short. Marty and his friends made their way through the line and

ONE YEAR EARLIER...

began to load the cars. Marty and Joe had decided to take the front car. After being strapped in, the train of cars began to lurch forward. Marty was so excited, he couldn't contain himself.

Up, up, up, they went. With each click clack of the climb, Marty's stomach came alive with butterflies. As they reached the peak of the first hill, Marty screamed, "This is it! This is it!" All of a sudden, everyone felt a quick jolt. The ride had stopped, and Marty and Joe were dangling over the edge of the first hill. Both boys were scared out of their minds.

36

Then, they heard a voice coming from a speaker within their car. "Please remain calm. The ride will continue in a few moments. Thank you for your patience."

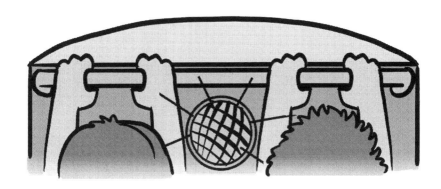

Patience?! Patience! Are you kidding me! We are about to plunge to our death! Oh, how I'll miss you, sweet cheese fries. God help us! I'm too young to die!!

Just then, they heard a loud pop, and the cars started moving. "We're saved! Yay, cheese fries!!!" Marty shouted as the coaster raced down the hill.

They continued to dive, climb, twist, and turn until the train of cars came to a stop at the loading dock. The sheer look of horror on their faces said it all. "That was the first and last time I'll ever get on the Cosmic Coaster," Marty declared. "Same," Joe agreed.

Chapter 6

Brain Freeze

After having lunch at the Pizza Planet, the group decided to ride something a little more calm. So, they got in line for the Asteroid Belt, which spins you around the sun. Speaking of the sun, it was getting really hot outside at this point. The kids waited in line for 20 minutes before getting on. The wind

felt wonderful once the ride started, and
it quickly dried their sweaty little bodies.
However, once the Asteroid Belt quit
turning, they were hotter than ever. Luckily,

they spotted a solution. "Look! Supernova

Snow Cones!" screamed Megan. The

children all squealed with delight. "I think

that's a great idea," said Mrs. Berry as she

directed them to the line. There were

different flavors, so it was very hard to choose. (Here's where you get to help them out. Choose any flavor or combination of flavors, and write them in the blanks if you own this book. If not, just pick the flavors in your brain without writing them.)

Lillie: I would like

_____, please.

Joe: I want _____.

Benny: I'll have half _____

and half _____.

Marty: Um... well... uh... how 'bout...

_____, _____,

_____, and a little

_____.

Megan: I think I'll have _____

with snow cream.

Mrs. Berry: And I'll have _____,

please.

Once the children received their snow cones, they quickly began to eat them. "Guys," Mrs. Berry said, "you need to slow down. You're going to get a brain freeze." "What's that?" Marty asked. Just then, a sharp pain hit

Marty right between the eyes. "Ow! Ow! Ow!" Marty exclaimed pinching the upper part of his nose. "Oh man, that really hurt!" Benny and Joe laughed with their bright colored tongues hanging out.

Chapter 7

Hold Your Breath!

Next, the group decided to head down to meet some of the Galaxy Rangers and get their autographs. "I've waited my whole life to meet The Master of Disaster!" Marty exclaimed. "Me too," said Benny. However, when they reached the character meet and greet, the line to get Master D's autograph was a mile long. There was a sign that read "60 minute wait." "We have to wait in line for an hour!!!" Marty cried. "You've got to be kidding me!" "Well, Joe and I are waiting,"

Benny replied. Marty just wasn't sure he would be able to have enough patience to stand there for that long. "Oh, ok," sighed Marty.

The minutes seemed to pass by like a kid waiting for Christmas morning. When they finally reached the front of the line, Marty could see his favorite TV character in the flesh. Marty's heart began to race, and his palms started sweating. Just then, the line worker brought a silver bar down in front of them and made an announcement. "I'm sorry. The Master of Disaster will be taking a break now and will return in 15 minutes." "What?! We're next! Master D, don't leave!!!" Marty shouted. "It's alright, Marty, calm down," Joe encouraged.

"I can't!" Marty screamed. "I've been standing in this line FOR-EV-ER! I don't think I'm going to make it!" "Maybe you should hold your breath and think about how awesome it's going to be when you get Master D's autograph," Joe suggested in hope that Marty would settle down. Marty took a deep breath and

closed his eyes. "Man," Benny said, "good job, Joe. He was losin' it!" A few minutes later, Marty started shaking and turning a little red. "Hold on, Marty," Joe encouraged. All of a sudden, the silver bar came up behind Marty, and Joe shouted, "Look! It's the Master of Disaster!"

At this, Marty released all the air he had been

holding and flew all the way back into

Master D.

"What is your name, earthling?" asked the Master of Disaster sternly. Marty looked up and stammered, "Um...uh...Mar...Marty."

"You have been on a great journey of patience, Marty, and I would like to reward you with a Blaster 5000," Master D said in a deep voice.

With that, the Master of Disaster handed Marty a ray gun. "Wow!" Marty exclaimed. "Thank you, Master D. Captain Marty takes no prisoners!!!" The Master of Disaster threw his head back and let out his evil laugh.

Chapter 8

Signs of Disaster

"Is it time for the Laser Launch next? We're running out of time, Mrs. Berry," Marty said with a worried look. "I think that ride is still pretty far away, Marty," replied Mrs. Berry, "but we can head that way." After passing by a number of rides, souvenir shops, and restaurants, the children began to grow tired. "How much farther?" asked Benny. "My legs feel like they're going to fall off!" "I think it's just ahead up this hill," Marty suggested. Huffing and puffing, they all reached the top panting. There in front of

them was a sign that read, "Laser Launch,"

and it had an arrow pointing to the right.

"What!!! I can't walk any further!" Marty exclaimed. "Save the drama for your mama!" Megan replied with disgust. "Come on, guys. It can't be much farther," Mrs. Berry encouraged. Five minutes later,

they arrived at the Laser Launch entrance.

Everyone stared in horror at what they saw.

"Marty? Uh...Marty?" Joe said shaking his

best friend's shoulder. "Aw, man. He's shut

down on us," Benny pointed out. The sign

read:

SORRY.... THIS RIDE TEMPORARILY CLOSED

"Marty's waited his whole life to ride the Laser Launch. It's just not fair," Lillie declared. "Well, sometimes life's NOT fair. I think Marty's handling this pretty well considering what a huge disappointment this is," Mrs. Berry replied. "Uh...Mrs. Berry...I don't think he's blinking or breathing," Megan pointed out.

Chapter 9

The Red Button

The group decided to head toward the gift shop before leaving the park. Marty was trailing behind them in a zombie-like state. He just wasn't the same after his dream to ride the Laser Launch was destroyed.

However, he soon realized he couldn't see anyone in his group anymore. He had been left behind. HE WAS LOST! "Where'd everybody go?" he worried. "What do I do? Where should I go?" Marty began to panic and weave in and out of the crowds of people.

"I should probably go to the front of the park where we came in," he thought. "However, I'm not sure I know the way." After about three different turns, Marty found himself down an alleyway in between 2 gift shops. "Oh man, what am I going to do?" he wondered. Just then, he caught a glimpse of

63

something shiny on the wall in front of him.
It was a large red button. "Hmm... I wonder
what this does?" he thought. "Buttons ARE
made to be pushed." Marty slowly lifted his

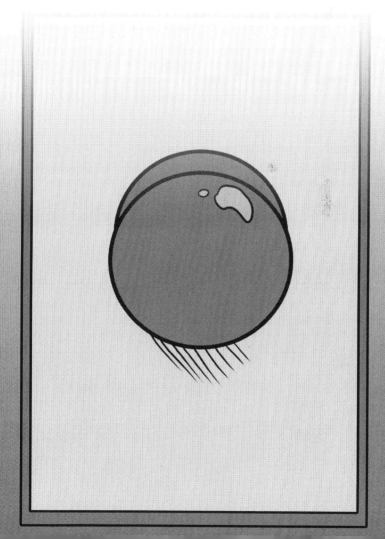

finger in a point position. He looked all around to see if anyone was watching. It was like an unseen force was pulling his finger toward the button, and he couldn't stop! Click.

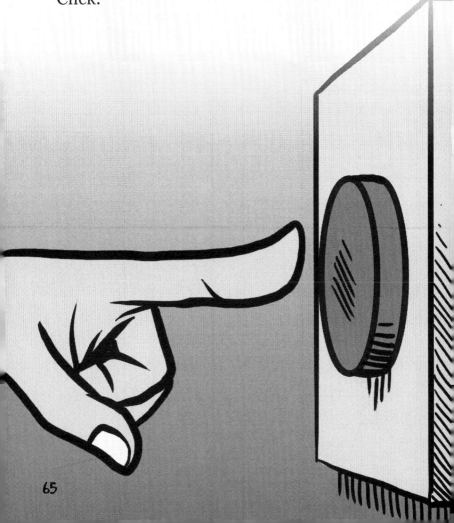

Rrrrrrer! Rrrrrrer! A loud alarm started

blasting his ears off, and Marty stumbled

backward into some trashcans. "Oh no!" he

shouted as he scrambled up and started to

run. When he reached the front of the
building, he saw people flooding out of the
Galactic Gifts store. Marty started to take off,
when he saw a familiar looking hat.

"Benny!" he hollered. "Hey, man! Where have you been? Mrs. Berry has been freaking out trying to find you," Benny explained. "Marty! There you are," Mrs.

Berry said trying to catch her breath.

Rrrrrrer! Rrrrrrer! The alarm continued to roar. "Where have you been?" she asked. "Um... here at Galactic Gifts," he said with a guilty look. "I guess I overlooked you. Come on. Let's round the others up and get out of

here!" she declared. Just then, the alarm stopped, and a worker appeared and made an announcement. "It's o.k. Someone pushed our emergency button. False alarm. You may reenter the store." "Dude, I bet that person is in big trouble!" Benny said. "Yeah, I bet he's gonna get it," Marty said with a smirk.

Chapter 10

Headed Home

"Guys, it's time to head up to the front to leave," Mrs. Berry said. All the kids let out a groan. "Do we have everyone?" she asked. "All present and accounted for!" declared Joe. They all began the long walk to the

front of the park. As Marty passed by each ride, he thought about all the situations he had gotten into that day. Just then, he saw the Galactic Cheese Fries sign. His mouth began to water. "Mrs. Berry...," Marty started. "No!!!" everyone shouted at the same time.

When they reached the front, classes were

getting on the bus. Everyone was sharing

and talking about all the excitement of the

day. "Have no fear! Marty is here!" he shouted to his classmates. Mr. Brown rolled his eyes. "Give me a break," sighed Megan.

As they drove away from Galaxy Zone, Marty took one last look out the window and whispered, "Until we meet again." Then, he

stood up and yelled, "Captain Marty takes no prisoners!!!" He shot his new Blaster 5000 up in the air over and over again. "Marty!" Mr. Brown shouted while glaring back in his mirror at him. "Sorry," Marty said slinking down into his seat. Then, without warning, everyone heard a loud burst.

The bus started slowing down. After it had

stopped, Mr. Brown got off to investigate.

The children started to get very loud and

excited at this new development. When Mr.

Brown returned, he said, "Well, we have a flat tire. We're going to have to wait until help arrives to change it. So, I need your patience." Just then, Marty spoke up. "I know all about this! Patience is how well you behave while you're waiting!" Mr. Brown

raised his eyebrows in amazement. "Don't worry, Mr. B. I've got this. I've had A LOT of practice." Marty kicked his legs up on the seat in front of him and put his hands behind his head and closed his eyes. "Marty, Marty, Marty, Mar-ty," he sang.

Alliteration

words that are next to each other or close together that begin with the same beginning sound

pg. 23 - At the food stand, Marty quickly ordered the large <u>gooey</u> <u>galactic</u> fries with extra cheese.

pg. 32 - "Man! The <u>Solar</u> <u>Splash</u> <u>soaked</u> me!" exclaimed Benny.

pg. 35 - With each <u>click</u> <u>clack</u> of the <u>climb</u>, Marty's stomach came alive with butterflies.

Now you try one!

terrible _____

(Think of a word with the same beginning sound.)

Don't read this page.
(You might learn something.)

BLACK HOLES are areas in space, where gravity is so strong that nothing, not even light, can escape from them. Black holes are thought to be formed by collapsed stars.

The **MILKY WAY** is the pale strip of light consisting of many stars that you can see stretched across the sky at night.

An **ASTEROID** is one of the very small planets that move around the sun between Mars and Jupiter.

References

Collinsdictionary.com. (2018). Asteroid definition and meaning | Collins English Dictionary. [online] Available at: https://www.collinsdictionary.com/dictionary/english/asteroid [Accessed 14 Aug. 2018].

Collinsdictionary.com. (2018). Black hole definition and meaning | Collins English Dictionary. [online] Available at: https://www.collinsdictionary.com/dictionary/english/black-hole [Accessed 14 Aug. 2018

Collinsdictionary.com. (2018). Milky Way definition and meaning | Collins English Dictionary. [online] Available at: https://www.collinsdictionary.com/dictionary/english/milky-way [Accessed 14 Aug. 2018].

More About the Author

After my first book came out, I began visiting different schools and speaking to them on how to become self-published and the value of dreaming. Marty has been traveling with me causing trouble...I mean...helping me.

Watch our school assembly video, and meet Marty at: **www.martyscrazyadventures.com**. Or, for further information, please email me at: christyharrisonclc@gmail.com

54739429R00062

Made in the USA
Columbia, SC
05 April 2019